Santa's Stray in

A Piano for Christmas

Written by Polly Basore

Illustrated by Carlene H. Williams

For Mom, who played piano while I danced.
— PMB

For my grandparents, the stories, the memories, the legacy.
— CHW

A Project of AngelWorks

First Edition

ISBN #0-9771749-1-3

Printed by Mennonite Press Inc., Newton, Kansas,
with book design by Larry G. Nichols II

Special thanks to The Lord's Diner of Wichita, KS for the use of the character, Simon.

Additional copies of "A Piano for Christmas" and "Santa's Stray," the original book in
this series, are available online from www.santasstray.org.

The story behind AngelWorks and the Santa's Stray series is told in the memoir,
"What Heaven Left Behind," available online at www.whatheavenleftbehind.com.

The world is a big place. Millions of children live in thousands of small towns and big cities. It is hard, even for Santa Claus, to keep track of every boy and girl. But Santa must keep track. He wants to know not just who is naughty and nice—but who is happy and sad. That's where Simon comes in...

Simon knew something was wrong when he could no longer hear the music.
Simon had heard the music every day after the children came home from school.
The sweet sound of experienced fingers playing a piano wafted up from a small house at the end of the street. Melodies spun their way through the air until reaching the highest tree branches where Simon lay, looking down on his neighborhood.

Simon didn't know much about the music. He didn't know the names of the songs or the composers or anything like that. But when he heard the music coming from the piano, it seemed to him the notes soared like birds, swirling up, swooping down, circling around, then flying apart, before finally coming back to land together, softly. The cat daydreamed of chasing the notes through the air.

One day, there was no more music.

Simon studied the house from his perch in the trees, trying to figure out why.

He watched people come to the house and park their cars. They wore dark colors. Delivery men stopped their trucks. They brought flowers to the door. Neighbors came out of their houses with baking dishes, covered in shiny foil. A constant stream of people went in and out of the little house for days.

And then it was quiet. Too quiet, Simon thought. He missed the music.

One afternoon, a little girl who lived in the house came out to sit on the steps. She sat by herself. The next day she came again. And the day after that. Sometimes she cried. Mostly she just sat and stared.

Simon worried about her. He crawled down from his tree and crept closer to her. A grasshopper jumped in the grass on her lawn. Simon leapt after it. He made a show of attacking the grasshopper, catching it midair, between his paws, hoping this would amuse the girl.

If it did, she didn't show it; the girl just stared straight ahead.

Simon kept trying. He saw a ladybug land on a dandelion. He arched his spine and crawled through the grass, stalking the small bug. But before Simon could pounce, the ladybug buzzed its wings and flew off, startling Simon, who fell over on his back.

When he got up and looked over at the porch, the steps were empty. The girl was gone.

Days went by, then weeks. Nothing seemed to cheer the little girl. Every day after school, she would sit on the steps by herself and stare ahead as the other children in the neighborhood went running and playing in their backyards along the creek.

"I don't feel like playing," she said when they asked her to join them.

Simon worried about this girl. She seemed so sad and lonely. And it seemed to him, the longer she was sad, the lonelier she became.

Simon wanted to help.

He used to think he wasn't good enough to help anyone, but that was before the night he'd met Santa, before Santa had asked Simon to belong to him.

"I need a cat who loves children as much as I do," Santa had said.

Santa had asked Simon to watch over the children and let him know whenever someone was sad or lonely or afraid.

Santa!

That night, Simon climbed up the highest branch on his tree and turned toward the North Star. He found his scratchy voice and meowed into the night with all his might.

Bre-owwwwwwww! Bre-owwwwwww!

To be honest, it was a horrible sound. In the neighborhood below, lights came on in the houses. People came out and shouted after the stray, "BE QUIET!" One man even threw a rolled newspaper, but Simon was too high for the paper to hit him.

Simon kept meowing toward the North Star. He meowed until dawn. *Bre-owwwwwwww! Bre-owwwwwww!*

When first light erased the stars from sight, Simon finally crept down to the lower branches and collapsed exhausted, into deep sleep.

"Simon... Simon..."

Still sleepy, Simon tucked his face under a paw and turned away from the voice calling his name.

"It's me, Simon. Wake up!"

Simon peeked below his paw and looked down. He saw the lengthening shadows and realized he'd slept most of the day. It was afternoon now.

At the bottom of the tree stood a balding man dressed in a red pullover sweatshirt, with the tail of a white tee shirt barely covering his enormous belly. He wore red shorts, too, with scrunched up gym socks and black high-top sneakers.

"Santa?!" Simon meowed to his friend.

"Yes, it's me," Santa said, eyes twinkling. "Come here, you noisy old stray, and tell me what's got you howling all the way to the North Pole."

Santa reached up toward Simon, who leapt into his arms and snuggled his face into the warm, familiar white beard before hopping down to walk alongside Santa's feet. The two walked the neighborhood, past the creek to the park where they found a bench to rest and talk. Passersby in the park heard only a cat's scratchy meow, but Santa, who speaks several animal languages, understood every word.

Simon told Santa about the small house at the end of the street, where the girl began sitting on the steps looking sad after the music stopped. The cat told about the people who came to the house, then the flowers and the baking dishes: "She's been sitting on the steps looking sad ever since. She sits there after school, and then goes inside only when her mother calls her for dinner. She says "no" when the other children ask her to come play, and I am afraid if she keeps saying no, they will stop asking!"

"Oh Simon, you are a wise cat," Santa said. "I am lucky to have you for a pet. And I am glad you called me. I think I know what is wrong. Let's go see her."

The old man and cat got up from their park bench and walked back across the creek, through Simon's neighborhood, past Simon's tree toward the small house at the end of the street.

There, a little girl sat on the porch looking lonely and sad.

Simon went up to her first, rubbing his fur against the girl's legs, back and forth and back and forth until finally she began to pet him. The old man approached next.

"I see you've met my cat."

"Stinky? I thought he was a stray," she said, staring ahead blankly.

"I prefer to call him Simon," the man said gently. "And your name is Sarah, right?"

"How did you know that?" the girl said, looking up at the man for the first time.

"Well, I knew your grandmother... Has she died?"

The girl stared silently, tears slowly replacing the blank look on her face. With her face turned upward, Simon could now look deep into her eyes and see what he had missed before: It was grief, the confusing mix of painful feelings that come when someone you love dies.

Simon didn't have much experience with grief. He wondered if Santa did. What could either of them possibly say or do to make this girl feel better? Simon sat down beside the girl to listen.

"Yes, she died a month ago," the girl said.

"And you miss her, don't you? Of course you do..." the old man said.

"Yes, I really do!" she said. "Grandma used to come over to my house to watch me after school. She would play the piano and I would dance and spin to the music. Sometimes I would get so dizzy I would fall down! And she would laugh. ..."

Simon noticed the girl almost smile as she recalled the memory. But her expression changed quickly.

"After she died, Mom put flowers and Grandma's picture on the piano. No one has played it since. And now it's so quiet in there after school...," she said, her voice trailing off.

"So quiet you have to come out here?" the old man asked.

"Yes."

He bent down on one knee to tie a shoelace that had come loose. While he was stooped over, he looked into the girl's face. She didn't appear to recognize him. He was in his workout clothes, after all. Santa decided it was just as well.

"Your grandmother wouldn't like it, you know," he said, "A piano not being played...."

"What's your name, anyway? And how did you know Grandma?" the girl interrupted. Simon curled his tail around his feet and wondered what Santa would say next.

"You can call me Nick," the old man replied. "I knew your grandmother when she was a little girl... "

"You don't look old enough to have known my grandma then," the girl interrupted again.

"Oh I am much older than I look," the old man said. "But I keep in shape," he said, patting his belly. Simon rolled his blue eyes.

"I knew her when she was a girl, alright. I remember she asked for a piano for Christmas every year! Your grandmother loved music. She would make up songs and sing, and dance just like you. She wanted a piano very much."

"Did Santa bring her one?" the girl asked hopefully.

"Well no, not exactly," Santa said, looking down as he searched for words to explain. "You see, your grandma's family was poor. And her parents said she couldn't have a piano — that their house was too small for a piano. At least that's what they told her. So Santa couldn't bring her a piano, because Santa doesn't go against parents' wishes, you understand?"

The girl nodded.

"But your grandma, she didn't give up. And neither did Santa. She kept asking for a piano and he kept looking for a way to give her one."

By this time, Simon had crawled into the lap of the girl who was petting him, as both listened eagerly to the old man's story.

"In time, Santa discovered there was a lonely widow who lived two houses from your grandmother. She had a piano, but what she longed for was the company of a child. She had no children or grandchildren of her own. She wrote to Santa asking if there wasn't something he could do.

He wrote back and told the old woman about your grandmother and suggested the old woman invite the child to come play her piano. Well, don't you know, the woman did so that very Christmas! And your grandmother went over to her house after school to play. She went every day until the woman died."

"The old woman died?!" the girl interrupted again.

Santa looked down at her kindly.

"Well yes, the woman died. It was years and years ago...."

"I'll bet Grandma was sad."

"Yes, she was. Just like you now. But the sadness doesn't last forever — not as long as the love and the memories," he said.

At that moment, the girl's mother called her to dinner. Before disappearing inside the house, she turned to the man in the red sweat suit and his black and white cat.

"Nick, thank you so much for telling me that story! Talking about her like that... well, it almost felt like she wasn't gone." The girl smiled brightly at them and waved good-bye.

"Well done, Santa," Simon said, after the girl was inside. "But how did you know?"

"How did I know what?" he asked.

"How did you know that talking about her grandma would make her feel better?" Santa scooped up the cat into his arms to explain.

"I am in the gift-giving business, Simon. And I have learned that the best things you can give someone aren't *things* at all.

"Go on..." purred Simon.

"When someone dies, those left behind need to talk. The most precious gift you can give is to listen, and to share in the stories that bring their loved ones to life."

And with that, Santa slipped Simon back up into his tree and disappeared into the twilight. Simon curled into a ball and went to sleep. And the neighborhood remained quiet until the next day, after school, when the sound of untrained fingers on piano keys filled the air.

The End

Polly Basore is founder of AngelWorks, a philanthropy committed to providing comfort and opportunity to those affected by poverty, homelessness, addiction or grief. This is her second book about Simon produced with Carlene H. Williams. Polly lives in Bel Aire, KS with her young son Henry and their six cats.

Carlene H. Williams is a freelance illustrator and art teacher. She holds a BFA in art illustration from Brigham Young University. In addition to the Simon series, she collaborated with her father, Roy E. Howard, on a book called "How the Music Came to Earth." She lives with her husband, Lucas, in Wichita, Kansas.

The proceeds from this book benefit Three Trees, Inc., a no-cost center that provides peer support services to grieving children and their families in Wichita, KS. Three Trees provides free services to hundreds of people each year. Please visit www.threetrees.org for information on how you can help children facing the loss of loved ones.